THE WALL IN THE MIDDLE OF THE BOOK

A book to share from
Scallywag Press

‘A book that celebrates
freedom of movement and thought.’

AMNESTY INTERNATIONAL

This paperback edition first published in 2019 by
Scallywag Press Ltd, 10 Sutherland Row, London SW1V 4JT

Published by arrangement with Dial Books for Young Readers,
an imprint of Penguin Young Readers Group, a division of
Penguin Random House LLC

Printed on FSC paper in Malaysia by Tien Wah Press

001

British Library Cataloguing in Publication Data available

978-1-912650-05-7

JON AGEE

THE WALL IN THE MIDDLE OF THE BOOK

Scallywag Press Ltd
LONDON

There's a wall in the middle of the book.

And it's a good thing.

The wall protects this side of the book . . .

from the other side of the book.

This side of the book is safe.

The other side is not.

But the most dangerous thing
on the other side of the book
is the ogre.

If the ogre ever caught me, he'd eat me up.

That's why I'm glad there's a wall
in the middle of the book,
and that I'm on this side of it.

Wait a second. What's going on?!

This is not supposed to happen
on this side of the wall!

Wow!
Thank you so much!

OH NO!
I'm on the other side of the book!

And you're the ogre who's going to eat me up!

Haw-haw-haw! I'm actually a nice ogre.
And this side of the book is fantastic!

Come on, I'll show you around!

Hey, ogre! Wait for me!

Praise for

THE WALL IN THE MIDDLE OF THE BOOK

' With too much attention toward outward threats, the knight neglects to see those from within—a timeless message but also one that, in 2018, will surely strike a chord with many readers. '

***Kirkus*, starred review**

'The message that walls don't help us understand our neighbors will stick.'

***Booklist*, starred review**

'As ever, Agee nails pacing and punch lines, making inventive use of the famous fourth wall as a literary device (and giving the book a new wall altogether). Most satisfying is his gentle reminder that preconceived notions about things and people, over a boundary or otherwise, are often distinctly wrong.'

***Publishers Weekly*, starred review**